Remember the Bible

Volume One

The simple, easy way to memorize your favorite Bible verses.

Table Of Contents

Remember The Bible

Forward by Kellie Ann Peterson

For many years I have been teaching and coaching families in crisis. In 2007 I began desperately searching for the answers to two major areas in which these families were continually struggling. The first was homework time. The second was having God's Word be the foundation for these families.

In 2009 I met Dave Farrow at a conference in New Mexico. After I heard him speak I looked at my husband and said, "God has just answered my prayer". The first thing I did was buy his Farrow Memory 6 CD Audio Kit™. At the end of the conference when Dave offered his audience the opportunity to become memory trainers, I literally raced over to him and said, "Sign me up!" I was certain that God had brought Dave Farrow into my life to answer the needs of so many families with struggling students.

When I got home doubt set in. I was scheduled to teach a group of parents the next day so I decided to listen to the first CD in the Audio Kit™ in order to teach it to my class. I thought if I could pull it off and they learned the memory techniques then I would know this really was from God and not some phony-baloney marketing trick. I was amazed at the results in my classroom the next day. Everyone increased their memory! Since that day I have taught many parents to use memory techniques so they can help their struggling students. One real-life example is the man in my class who learned the memory techniques for spelling. After he applied the memory technique to his spelling word he stood up in front of the entire class and spelled it. He told them, "I have never been able to spell, not in my whole life, and now my son needs help with his spelling." He paused and as tears rolled down his face he told the class, "Now I can help my son!" It is the most incredible life experience to see God reach down from Heaven using memory techniques and changing the families of the world.

I was so excited using Dave's memory techniques that I almost forgot the second great need for families. Until one day when I was working with a mom who needed God to help her through a possible life-or-death situation with her ex-husband. I knew law enforcement would not be able to fully protect her if her ex was intending to hurt her. However, I know the Word of God is powerful. With a humble heart I sought God and asked Him to show me the Bible verses she needed to be safe and protected. He answered my prayer and I went straight to her home that morning and taught her the verses using memory techniques. Those scriptures saved her life! Her ex showed up on drugs one night and struck her to the ground. She told me as she was falling she knew he was going to really hurt her this time. She said, "Then, all of a sudden, I remembered the verses. As they ran across my mind I mumbled them to myself. My ex looked at me in a strange way and said 'I'm out of here!' For the first time ever he stopped hitting me after the first strike."[1] She has never been hit again!

Memorizing the Word of God is powerful! When Dave asked me to co-write this book I was so excited I did not sleep for days. It is an incredible honor for me to serve our Heavenly Father this way. My desire is to be able to help God's children all over the world know His Word!

*Due to the issue of confidentiality I am not able to give names or specific details to protect the identity of my clients.

Kellie Ann's Dedication:

To

Avinu Malkenu,

My Father My King

Remember The Bible

Forward by Dave Farrow

In my 15 plus years of experience doing memory training, speaking and interviews, people have asked me about memorizing religious scripture again and again. Each time I was asked it felt like it wasn't the right time to do it. Then the day came where I stopped for a moment and looked back at my career to see how much I have written. I wanted so much to leave a legacy of something meaningful. I'm the only person in my generation to actually invent new memory techniques and take on challenges trying to apply memory techniques to all sorts of situations that people thought could never be applied to, like dance, martial arts moves, or musical scores, but when it came to memorizing religious scripture I always felt that I didn't have a right to write a book on it because I'm not a religious scholar. That is, until several of my students came up to me and asked me point blank to do this. I've always had a calling and a huge desire to do so but I wanted to approach the subject with a level of humility and understanding, so I went on a search for someone I could write this book with; somebody who is skilled with memory techniques and who is also a scholar and theologian. When I met Kellie Ann, I knew I had found my cowriter. In this book I'm good at taking you through a step-by-step formula to memorize any group of text, be it scripture, speeches, prose or technical material. This technique is amazing and I really enjoy teaching it. It will give you the ability to commit vast amounts of words to memory.

That's how I felt when I started this project, that this was an intellectual challenge and another opportunity for me to stretch memory techniques to something more practical than demonstrations on stage. Then something unexpected happened. The word started to come alive for me and I started to appreciate scriptures that I never appreciated before. I started to really understand it as I was committing it to memory and I began to enjoy it on a whole new level.

I am very happy and proud to bring you this volume and I hope it brings to you an understanding and joy for the word of the Bible in the same ways that brought me a deeper understanding and enjoyment of the scripture.

It slices, it dices, it memorizes scripture!

The first time I was asked to teach someone how to memorize Scripture was in the most unlikely of places - the Shopping Channel! Memory techniques and memory training have long been a mainstay of shopping channels and infomercials. It's a tough business and a tough job to get up in front of millions of people and simply have a 24 hour commercial. Of course I wasn't given 24 hours for myself, I was given barely a half hour to make my case. As I was telling people the benefits of memorizing people's names and languages, cutting their study time in half, overcoming the ADHD issues and using the power of the mind, the host asked me, "What about memorizing scripture?" And I responded that the techniques would work for any text, Scripture included, and it would be simple and easy to memorize any amount of Scripture that you like to remember.

I received many responses from my time on the Shopping Channel. Many people asked me about education for their kids with ADHD and how I overcame it, and many other education questions. But the few seconds spent mentioning scripture memorization on the air lead to a wave of people e-mailing me questions. Each e-mail had different scriptures in it and each person asked me to help them memorize it.

Today, I understand the reason for that tremendous response. People want to remember the word because people want to make it a part of them; they want to be able to quote it, mention it and refer to it at times when they need it. To give strength. Well, my friend, look no further. my mission with this book is to give you all the tools that you need to not just understand and read but to truly remember the word of God.

Dave's Dedication:

To

Mom

Chapter One: How Your Memory Works

Often when people think of memorizing something they try to repeat it over and over. We all know that doesn't work. It is difficult, time consuming and usually we end up forgetting it in the end. Other people might try singing in the shower in the shower or trying something else.

There is a better way. I lecture at colleges all across the country teaching this stuff so it really works. This is an entire science and art form that dates back thousands of years to the ancient Greeks. I am the current Guinness World Record Holder for Greatest Memory so rest assured that I have worked with everyone from all ages and all walks of life so I can say with authority, you can do this! You really have a powerful memory, you just don't know how to use it.

Getting Started

I have found that the best way to get started using these techniques is to start with the basics. Once you learn this I believe you will open your eyes to the powerful memory you really do have naturally.

So lets get started with this fun game. The following is a list of objects used in a normal memory test. The test consists of a list of ordinary objects in a specific order. Users read the list and try to recall it. The average person can recall 5-6 out of 10. If you can reach 8 you are at the genius level.

But we are going to do this differently. Read my story and imagine it in your minds eye. As you do you will be taking the first step to unlocking your naturally powerful memory.

The Story

First imagine a welcome mat to your front door, and someone draws all over it with a marker. Imagine it being ruined by graffiti. I would remember that. Now imagine that you really want to wash it off so you use lukewarm water to wash it with. Yes it is that simple. You try hard and it is not working so you need some help. You bring in John Wayne! That's right, he is the next item in the list. John Wayne is pouring water all over this mat. The next step in the list is actually an acting class, so imagine John Wayne going back to acting school. That would make the news for more reasons than one. The next item in the list is a Roman legion, so I imagine John Wayne dressed as a Roman like in the movie, "The Greatest Story Ever Told."

Now for a quick review. What is the first item in

the list? A mat. Then marker is drawn on it and then lukewarm water to wash it with, and then we have John Wayne, then acting class, then Roman soldier.

The next item is an apple core. I think you understand the game so far and we are almost done. Imagine the Roman soldier eating an apple or putting it on the end of their spear. Next is a sea gull. Imagine a bunch of sea gulls stealing the apples from the Roman.

You may be wondering what the point of this story is. Well, inside this story is a list of objects. This list is important but we will get to that later. Right now lets just see how many things on the list you recall.

Without reading the story above, write down the list you just memorized. Make sure you visualize the story and go step by step.

1. ____________	5. ____________
2. ____________	6. ____________
3. ____________	7. ____________
4. ____________	8. ____________

How did you do?

My guess is you did great.

If you got 8 items right then you have reached a genius level. Try this with kids. It is a fun game that helps you improve your memory. There is one more reason to try this game with kids. The list will help them remember the first books of the New Testament. Think about it. Mat is for Mathew, marker is for Mark and lukewarm water is for Luke, and so on. Enjoy this game. Practice it with other lists and you will strengthen your memory.

How To Memorize Words And Scripture

Keywords

When memorizing any vast amount of text, there is actually a shortcut that was discovered by experts thousands of years ago. Even though the shortcut is really important and very useful, I still see people making this mistake constantly, so here's your first lesson on memorizing scripture:

In order to memorize every word you don't have to memorize it word for word!

The first response I get from people when I say this is "huh?" What I mean by this phrase is that even if you want to memorize something word for word, your brain will never commit to memory every single word because it doesn't have to. When you read this sentence, generally your brain will skip over words it has encountered often enough and that it doesn't feel are necessary to sound out or repeat. So when you are memorizing a speech, you don't have to memorize the words if, the, at, a, of, in order to grasp the meaning of the entire sentence. Compare this to the job of an actor onstage: when an actor forgets a line, someone from stage right or stage left tries to prompt them, but they don't repeat the entire line. They generally repeat the first few words of the line and those words will remind the person of the entire sentence. It is the same with memorizing scripture. I am not suggesting you skip words or disregard them. All I'm showing you is a simple shortcut that will cut your work down to one 20th of what it would be if you tried to memorize every single word.

So, the shortcut is called keywords. A keyword is a word that will remind you of the entire sentence. Because of this, everybody will pick different keywords that will help them remember the entire sentence.

For example, take the phrase: "Yea, though I walk through the valley of the shadow of death, I will fear no evil: for thou art with me."

If you are trying to remember that particular phrase it is most likely you would not remember the entire phrase all at once. Some words would stand out. Perhaps the words "walk" and "shadow of death" stand out to you. These words stand out because they are very striking visual images and as a result, very easily remembered. When you're trying to memorize a phrase like this, it is useful to pick out the key words that would remind you of the entire sentence. Once you can remember those key-words, the rest of the sentence will fall right in your head as if you have it written on the inside of your eyelids. Talk about an interesting visual!

Go through the following examples we have selected and choose some keywords in each line of Scripture that will be the most likely to trigger your memory for the rest of the sentence. Keep in mind that this is a very personal art form. What I mean is that you may choose different keywords than we will. That is perfectly fine and in fact, I encourage you to think about the keywords that you would choose for yourself, ones that help to give you power over the technique and will help you remember the phrase even better.

Substitute Words

Picking out the keywords is an excellent technique that will cut down your work tremendously. You really go through 10, even 20 times the amount of words and memorize it all by using the shortcut. But that's all it really is, a shortcut, not truly a memory technique. The following is one of the oldest and most well tested memory techniques on the planet and it's called Substitute Words. This technique dates back over 2000 years and was first accredited to the ancient Greeks but there is also some evidence that ancient China and ancient India have a history of this technique as well. It is only now, in this age and this generation that we have the technology to understand why the technique works so well.

In essence, it uses a part of your brain that looks for patterns. Every waking moment, every place you go, everything you see, and every piece of information you encounter is being compared to every other piece of information in an effort to find patterns. Looking for and finding patterns, is a survival mechanism for our brains. The brain that can find patterns is the brain that can predict patterns and there is no greater survival mechanism than the ability to predict what's going to happen next in life. Memory experts like me have taken advantage of this mechanism of our brain for thousands of years and here's how it works: remember back to a time where you were looking at a tile floor or some sort of pattern on the wall that was repeating. After a while you may become bored and stare at this pattern. Your brain will start to see other patterns within this random pattern. A series of checker boards to your mind will turn into exes and squares and lines - if this happens to you, you're not crazy, I assure you! This is the normal response to a healthy brain when it encounters a random pattern. The same thing happens when we look at clouds. I have never looked at a cloud and not seen something else like teddy bear, bunny rabbit, or a giant hydraulic compressor (okay maybe I just like technology too much).

Even though I made a joke about seeing a giant hydraulic compressor in a cloud formation, there is actually an important point in that. That part of our brain that tries to find patterns will only find patterns that we are used to looking for. Because I really enjoy technology and mechanical things, I'm always looking for technology and mechanical objects, and it is very easy for me to see objects like these. As the disclaimer on the television set says, "Individual results may vary."

So what does this have to do with memorizing scripture? Just because you can take a line of Scripture and break it down into its keywords doesn't mean you've memorized it yet. To take it further, you still have to take those words and link them together using memory techniques as I've shown you how to do. Link together words that you can visualize. But can you guess how substitute words fit into this? When you encounter a word that you cannot visualize but you have to memorize, you can simply employ the substitute word technique! When you use the Substitute Word technique, you are in essence speaking your brain language. Your brain wants to memorize things using images and sensory input. By translating these complex sounding words into objects and images you can easily retain them and memorize them for as long as you want.

To Review:

Step one - pick out the keywords

Step two - turn the words that are not visual into something you can visualize using a process called substitute words

Step three - link these words together just like you did that original list of objects

Step four - repeat as necessary

Well, now you've heard all the theory and there's really nothing left but the word. On the next pages you will be shown a line of meaningful scripture and then you will be given a description of how to memorize it on the right. You don't need to use our image every time but it is the right place to start. At first the images seem weird, but over time you will start to feel the images helping the information stick in your brain. The more you do it the easier it becomes. It is now time to memorize the word, so let's get started!

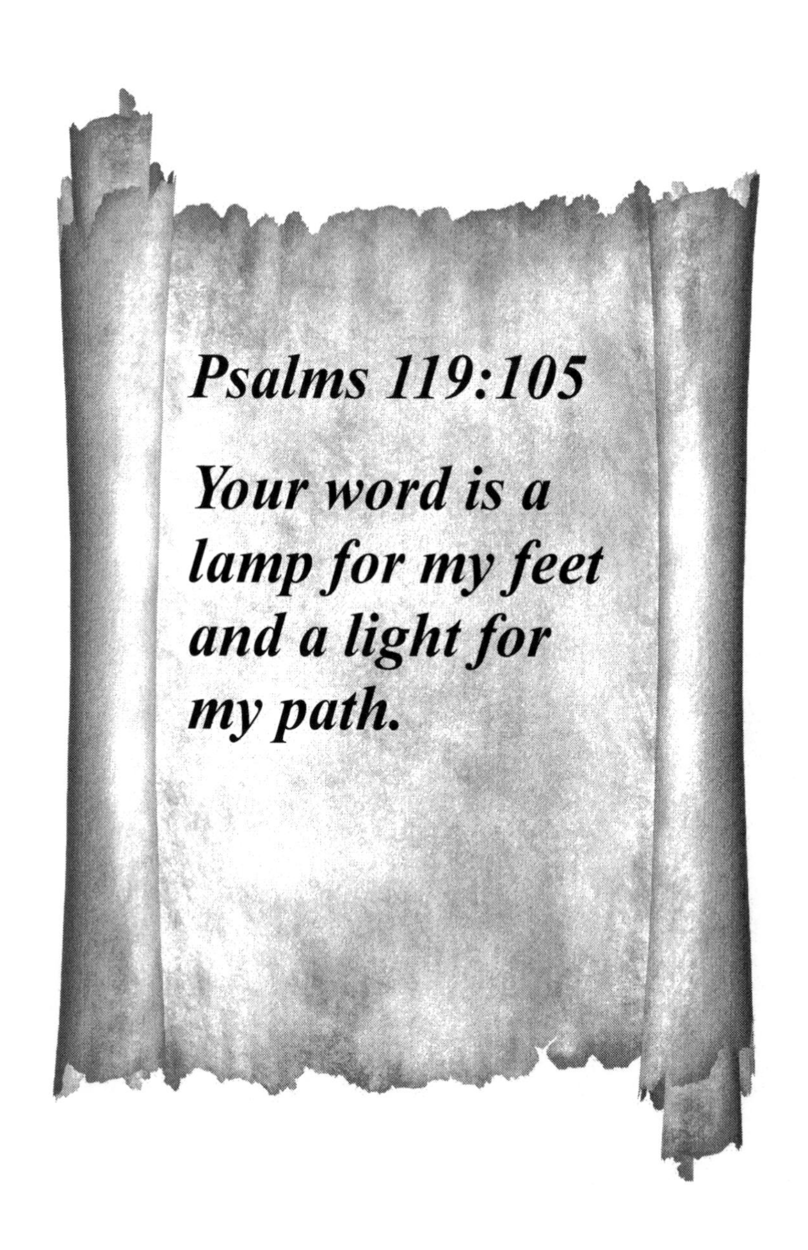
Psalms 119:105
Your word is a
lamp for my feet
and a light for
my path.

TOPIC: Word of God

*“Your **word**”*

To Memorize: Picture a Bible book similar to a cartoon character with arms, legs and sneakers (aka mini-wheat TV commercial or Psalty the Singing Song Book). It has a huge label on it that says, “Word”.

I used the personification (where you imagine something coming alive) linking step here by giving it arms and legs because the Word of God is so alive to me. Another idea could be to see the letters in an exaggerated size or add action by seeing the word “word” doing some type of action to prepare to turn a light/lamp on.

*“is a **lamp**”*

The Bible is holding a very large lamp.

The picture I saw here was an old train type lantern being waved by the conductor as he went by. As a kid I used to see that in movies and I always thought wow, it has to be the biggest lamp I ever saw. I always assumed it probably weighed 100 pounds. Another idea could be seeing a lighthouse or an exaggerated version of a regular house lamp. Maybe your house lamp becomes as large as a lighthouse?

"For ***my feet"***

and He puts it down in front of my feet

In this part of the picture I personalized the link by making it my feet. Maybe you would like to make it huge clown feet or your feet in your favorite dream shoes?

"And a ***light for my path"***

and with each step I take my path lights, or it lights my path, or it is so bright it makes a light for my path

At first I saw train tracks ahead of me being lit by the light but then remembering how difficult it was to walk on train tracks at night and how often I twisted my ankle, I decided that I had better make it a dirt path that is all smoothed out with no pot-holes! Another option might be that you see a path through a jungle or a city. Maybe your path has adventures and dangers on it and the light helps you become aware of them. Another idea might be that you see the word "path" and it lights up as you walk on it.

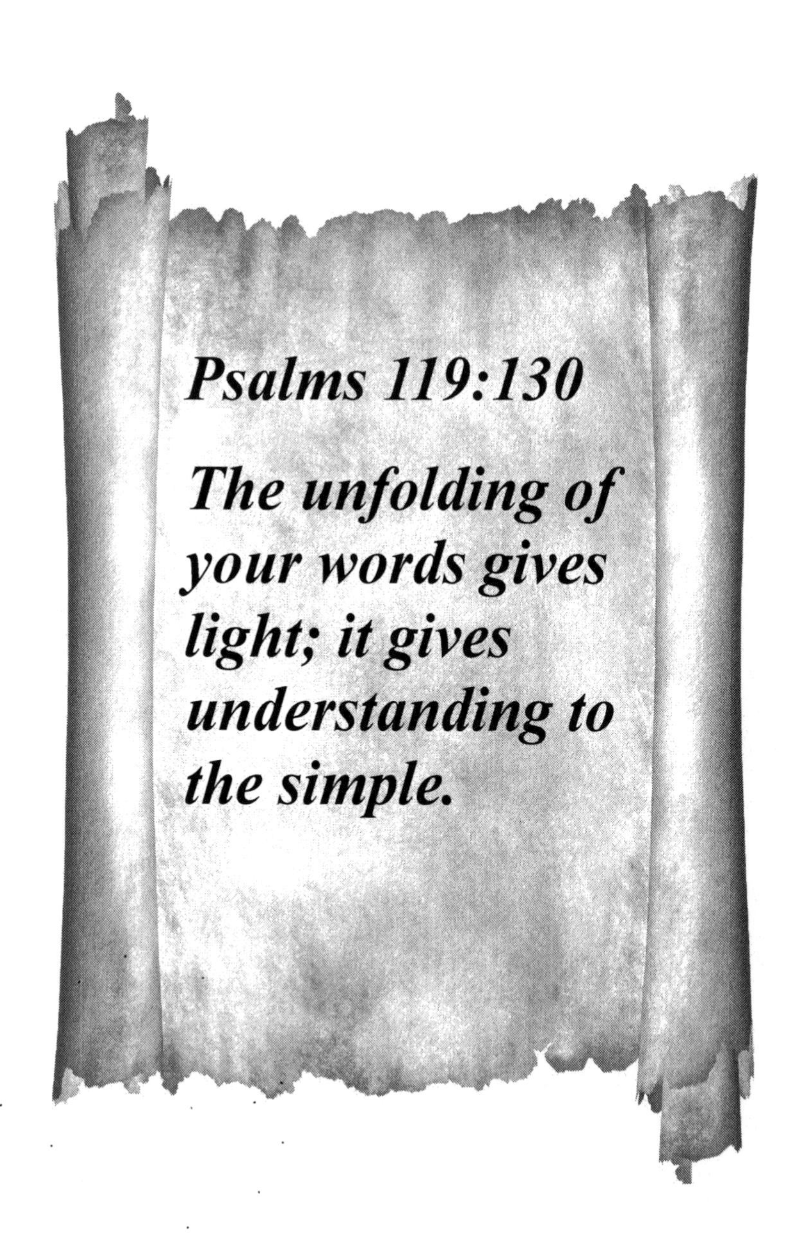
Psalms 119:130
The unfolding of your words gives light; it gives understanding to the simple.

TOPIC: Word of God

"The **unfolding** of your **words**"

Picture a huge pile of words that you have to unfold. As you unfold the words

When I visualized this I saw a huge pile of words, similar to a laundry basket full of clothes. The words are all folded together in a mess and I had to unfold them so they can become clear. Another thought is to picture a big origami structure made of words that you have to unfold. Or possibly you want to go with the previous picture of a whole bunch of Bibles with arm and legs with huge labels on them that say "Word" that are all tangled together and you have to unfold them. Originally I tried to go with this picture but I kept coming up with the issue of folding and not unfolding.

"gives **light**"

while unfolding light rays shoot out, like fireworks, giving light.

I literally saw an opening similar to a window looking out into a beautiful sky, while I am unfolding the words. Through that opening coming right towards me were rays of light that shot past me like fireworks. Perhaps you see a search type light that goes up into the sky or shines down on you. Or perhaps as you unfold the Bibles with arms and legs the "Word" labels gives light, similar to glowing in the dark.

"it gives **understanding** to the **simple**"

As the light shoots past your head you can hear it saying, "Understanding is simple, understanding is simple"

My memory link here is very auditory in hearing the fireworks shooting past my ears saying understanding is simple. I can hear this in a rhythm almost musically. Other types of learners may instead picture a simple person having an instantaneous moment of enlightenment, "I GET IT!" "I understand now!" "That was simple!" The stronger the emotional response or humor the easier it is to recall later.

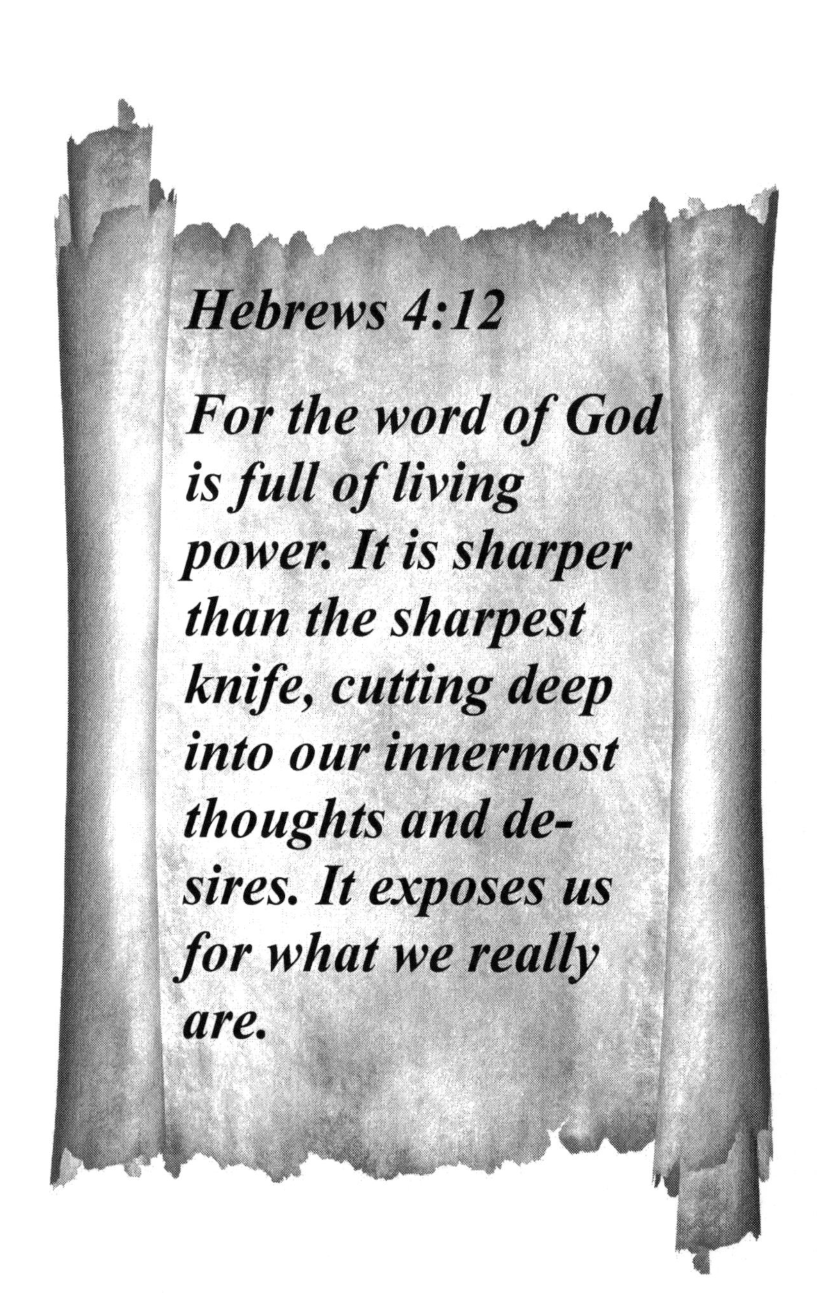
Hebrews 4:12
For the word of God
is full of living
power. It is sharper
than the sharpest
knife, cutting deep
into our innermost
thoughts and de-
sires. It exposes us
for what we really
are.

TOPIC: Word of God

*"For **the word of God**"*

Picture an enormous Bible, the cover reads "THE WORD OF GOD"

This can be the same picture of the Bible with arms and legs with the label "the Word of God" on it. For the purpose of consistency, I went with the already established picture of the Bible cartoon character labeled the Word of God. However, I have linked this verse personally to a long term association of envisioning Jesus sitting on His white horse as described in Revelation 19:11-16. This verse describes Jesus' return with the armies of heaven, preparing for war. Revelation 19:13 reads, "His name is the Word of God". This was the first image that came to my mind and is a very powerful and almost shocking image for me. Using powerful, shocking images when they are the first image that pops into your head is very important. Your brain has already made that a long term memorable link or image. Therefore, it will be easier to recall it later.

"is full of living power"

When it opens it is full of lightning bolts of living power that shoot out

What I picture here is every time the enormous Bible opened it was full of lightning bolts with jagged edges and enough power to light up New York City.

Maybe you have an impression of something else that reminds you of living power like seeing a nuclear reactor plant full of power.

*"It is **sharper than the sharpest knife**"*

The jagged edges of the living power lightning bolts are sharper than the sharpest knife

Perhaps you see an action similar to the old commercial about Ginsu knives cutting a nail and then a tomato to show that it is the sharpest knife. Or some type of image that means knife or sharpest knife to you.

*"**cutting deep** into our **innermost thoughts and desires**"*

the sharpest knife is cutting into a HUGE sign that says, "innermost thoughts and desires" the sign looks like the "Hollywood" sign, as seen on TV.

I saw a huge Samurai sword coming out of Heaven cutting the sign in half and the top half fell forward. I could hear the noise of cutting metal and the crashing noise as it fell. My example is once again auditory. A visual person may see the sharpest knife image change into a chainsaw and cutting into the sign. Or, possibly you may want to make an emotional connection by personally experiencing the cutting deep of your innermost thoughts and desires, straight to your heart.

*"It **exposes us for what we really are"***

The sign crashes down, exposing us standing behind the sign

I visualized myself standing behind this sign when it falls. I was exposed because I was hiding there eating a whole box of chocolates or some type of image you conjure up when thinking of the phrase, exposing us for what we really are.

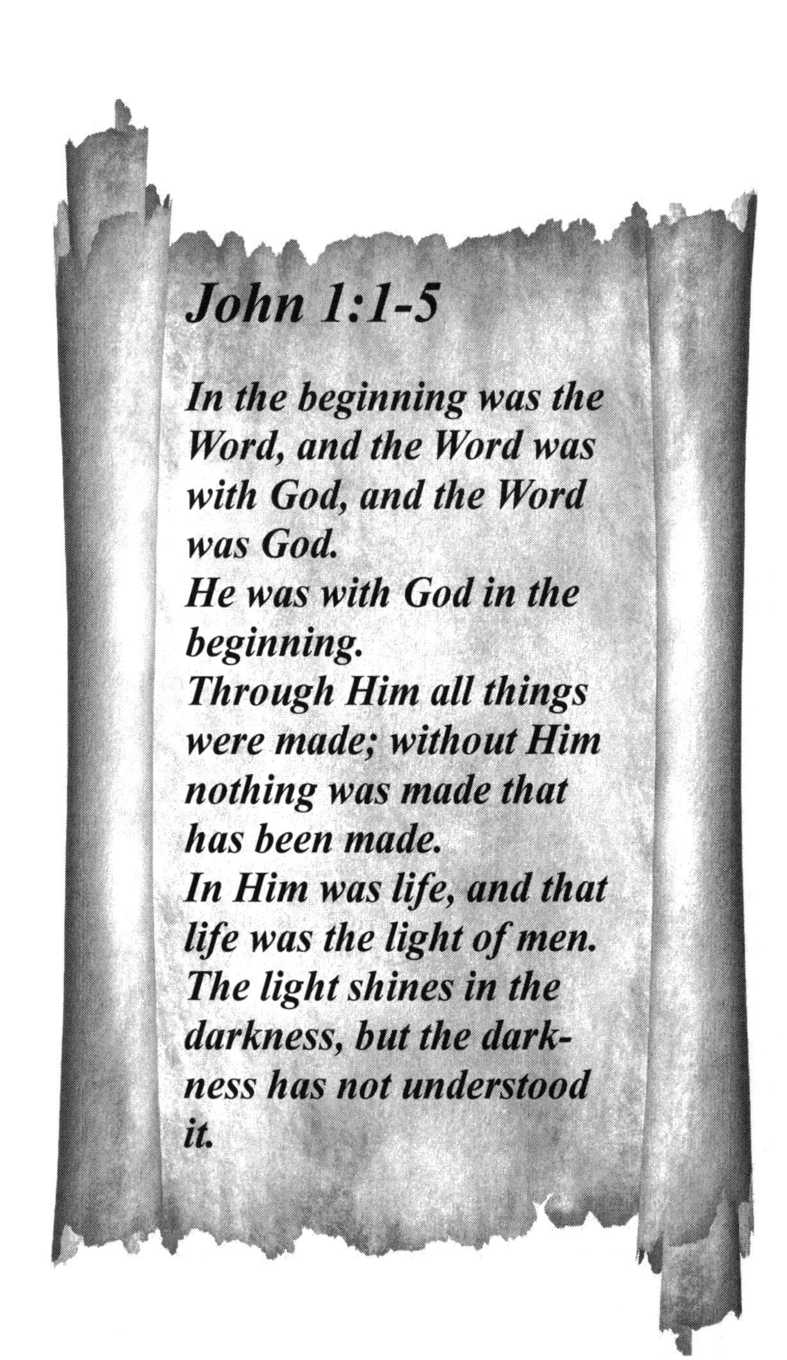
John 1:1-5
In the beginning was the Word, and the Word was with God, and the Word was God.
He was with God in the beginning.
Through Him all things were made; without Him nothing was made that has been made.
In Him was life, and that life was the light of men.
The light shines in the darkness, but the darkness has not understood it.

TOPIC: Word of God

"*In the **beginning***"

Picture a starting line, e.g., as in a marathon race

This is the first scripture I tried to memorize. Because it is hard to visualize these phrases Dave helped me by using a substitute word picture, i.e. of running a race. When he came up with that picture, I realized his idea was brilliant, it matches the themes in the New Testament, thus I start my visualization there too. However, if this does not work well for you, take some time and focus on the word "beginning" and go with whatever first pops into your mind. Some ideas I have heard are having a baby, or possibly the beginning reminds you of Creation.

"*was the **Word***",

Picture a Bible book similar to a cartoon character with arms, legs and sneakers (aka mini-wheat TV commercial or Psalty the Singing Song Book). It has a huge label on it that says, "Word".

The difficulty with the next few phrases is that the word "Word" is used in multiple ways, with different meanings, and as different people. As you create links or use substitute words try to go with something that can change or adjust to the next phrase with clarity. This is the reason why I went with the personification memory link option. Personifying the word "Word", making Him a person, made it easier for me to transition through the different meanings and people he is referred to.

*"and the **Word** was **with God**"*

God is the Word's running coach; Word and God shake hands

My visualization here has people in the stands, runners stretching next to the Word, who also is stretching and has on running shoes. Over on the sideline is God. He has on a coach's jersey and a stop watch in his hand. When the Word sees Him out of the corner of his eye he walks over. God puts out his hand and they shake hands while God tells Him encouraging words about how he will be with Him during the race. This picture has strong emotional meaning for me the thought of God standing by me while I run the race of my life and Him saying he will be with me is very emotional. Having strong emotional responses or feelings strengthen the memory link.

*"and the **Word was God**."*

God and Word hug each other, coming together, becoming one

What I see here is similar to someone standing a

good distance away from two people who hug. At this distance they look as though they are one image. Another idea may be seeing the Word turn into God and then change back to help remember the past tense, was God.

"He was"

Word - Bible book cartoon character wearing a t-shirt with the words "HE WAS" flashing on the front of it

Originally I did not have a link for "He was". However, the first few times I taught it I had people in the audience who missed this phrase. So I asked them how they would link it. They came up with the Word cartoon character wearing a t-shirt with a flashing "He Was" on the front of it. Using their idea has helped many since then. A common way I use to denote past vs. present is to imagine something to the left of the item. So he was is to the left of the next item. This is a good way to imagine time in memory linking.

"with God"

Word and God shake hands

Once again I see my Word cartoon character turn and shake hands with God and God is wishing Him well. Again if this does not work for you focus on the phrase "with God" and go with the first thing that comes to your mind. Because that will the first thing that comes to your mind the next time you recall this information.

"in the beginning."

Looking back again at the starting line, e.g., as in a marathon race

Here I see the Word turn and go up to the starting/beginning line and take His position to start the race. If you chose another image for the beginning, use it here as well. The continuity of the same picture each time helps enhance the memory recall.

"Through *him* ***all things were made;"***

Breaking through the tape at end of race (as in winning a race). Imagine Jesus with tools in his hands standing before a humongous work bench, looking at all the things that were made or creating all the things that were made

Hearing the gun go off and crowd cheering I envision the Word (which I now see as Jesus) breaking through the tape stretched across the starting/beginning line. This was the only image I had for the word through. Other people have suggested Him running through a tunnel. "All things were made" is an interesting abstract phrase. What if you could imagine every person, animal and plant had a stamp on them that read made by Jesus, similar to made in China.

*“**without him NO-thing** was made that has been made.”*

Workbench covered with Ø Ø Ø Ø Ø’s = international symbol for “NO”, like “No-thing”, has been made

In this phrase I took the word nothing and changed it to a substitute word no-thing which created a better image for me. No-thing instantly conjured up the image of a no parking sign. Sometimes breaking a word apart will help develop better substitute words.

*“In him was **life**, and that life was the light of men.”*

The symbol Ø rotates up and grows and becomes the planet Earth rotating on its axis and Jesus grows bigger than the planet and leans over and he breathes life in to the planet, i.e., plants and animals and the men light up like light bulbs!

What I envisioned here was the Ø symbol lifting off of the sign and becoming like a huge earth balloon which Jesus took in his hands and began to breathe into it. This is an incredible image for me because it instantly linked to the images described in Ezekiel

37:1-10. Ezekiel was standing in a valley of dead bones. The Bible says, “and breath entered them; they came to life and stood up on their feet- a vast army”. This is certainly a story in the Bible that gives a vivid picture of God breathing life into humans.

*“The **light** shines in the **darkness**,”*

The Ascension of Jesus, with light rays radiating from His hands, the rays covering the Earth like the rising sun, chasing away the darkness.

When I was a child there was a very special place I would go in the morning right before the sun would come up. I could see the sun coming over the hill and cascading onto the ground, as though a line of sunlight was taking over the cold and darkness of night. I frequently tried to out run the sun rays as they came towards me. Perhaps light shining in the darkness looks very different to you; for example a lighthouse, a candle, a search light on a car or a boat or a light switch.

*“but **the darkness** has not **understood** it.”*

The darkness - the black void of space filled with question marks ? ? ? ? ? ? ? instead of stars, retreating from the light

rays, saying, “What is it?, I don’t understand.”

Another variation for this phrase, people looking at the light bulb that Thomas Edison made and not understanding what it is. This would also be a great place to use personification. Imagine the darkness as a living being made of oil or black powder. Then it will look at it in a quizzical way and not understand.

Jeremiah 29:11
"For I know the plans I have for you," declares the Lord, "plans to prosper you and not to harm you, plans to give you hope and a future.

TOPIC: Work

*"For **I know the plans I have for you," declares the Lord,"***

Picture the Lord as an architect, who is unrolling the architectural plans of your life with multiple pages, "I know the plans I have for you" declares the Lord as he looks at you.

Picking out words in the phrase that you can easily find a mental image for is the goal here. I went with the keyword plan. Because it instantly reminded me of Psalms 139:16 "All the days ordained for me were written in your book before one of them came to be." I always pictured God opening up a book that has my name on it. While looking at me, He starts our conversation with this verse, "for I know the plans I have for you..." I linked this verse to the other verse because it has a very important personal image for me. Maybe you visualize something entirely different like a woman in my audience did. She saw parents sitting at a kitchen table making plans for their child's college funds. You may want to add more details about their lives in general.

*“**plans** to **prosper** you*

He unrolls the first page of the plan and a HUGE pop-up word jumps out that says prosper in flashing lights”

Her story continued with the parents creating the plan for their child. They write “prosper” on a piece of paper. It turns into money and starts to multiply. It keeps multiplying until the whole room is filled with money. Other great visuals here might be finding the pot of gold at the end of the rainbow, winning the lottery, or possibly having a home full of children.

*“And **not** to **harm** you,”*

The Lord flips to the next page and on it there is a bright yellow caution sign, which reads “No Harm”

Going with the above parent story you may see the parents running around in a crazy manner looking for a safe to put the money in so no harm comes to it. What comes to your mind when you think of, not to harm you? Maybe you see or feel the protection of a loving parent, police, fireman, a security alarm, or a warm coat on a cold day. Personalizing is one way to link this. Maybe you want to add action like some one trying to harm you and God intervenes in some way and stops it. Or you see a sign on yourself or someone else that reads “not to harm you” instead of “kick me”.

*“plans to give you **hope**“*

above the “no harm” sign is a huge rainbow stretching across the sky that spells out the word HOPE

Another idea here could be receiving a set of plans that give you hope. I picked the word hope and future as two separate keywords. Others have put them together.

*“and **a future**”*

And in the O of the word Hope is a door that opens to a future

I envisioned myself walking up to this huge letter “O” in the rainbow and opening the door. As I looked in I saw my future, not like fortune telling, more like a future with God in Heaven, surrounded by love and beautiful things.

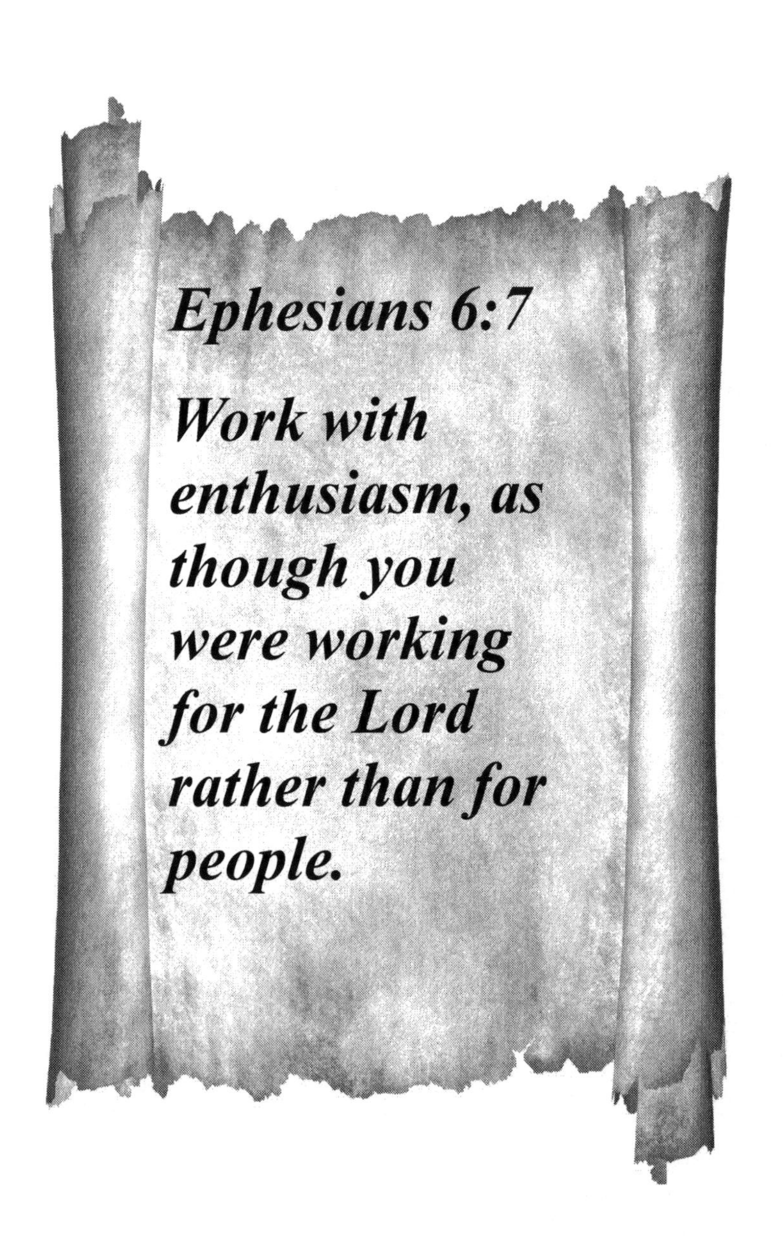
Ephesians 6:7
Work with enthusiasm, as though you were working for the Lord rather than for people.

TOPIC: Work

"***Work*** *with* ***enthusiasm***"

You are at work and the word enthusiasm is running across your desk. Imagine it like a big letter N, ...N thooose!

I took the keyword enthusiasm and personified it by allowing it to sing. I added action having it run across my desk. Below is a parallel story from a visual learner. She personalized and exaggerated to make better links. She saw a crane operator working to move the word enthusiasm which looked like a very tall building.

"As though you were working for the Lord"

The letters are singing, "working for the Lord, working for the Lord"

Continuing on, our visual learner changed her visual focus to the big brawny crane operator that is moving the word enthusiasm. He was wearing a pink t-shirt with the words "working for the Lord" in silver letters. Her story became humorous by visualizing the crane operator dressed in something that was way out of the ordinary.

“Rather than ***people****”*

And you sing back, “not people, not people”

Her story continues with her still focusing on the crane operator while he’s “working for the Lord”. Then the crane operator looks down towards his co-workers and he sees that he is surrounded by dogs and cats in hard hats, rather than people. Once again humor was used by envisioning something far outside of the norm, increasing the power of the memory link. If the words on the shirt don't remind you of working, imagine doing the activity like digging a hole with a hard hat on. Pick an object or action that reminds you of working.

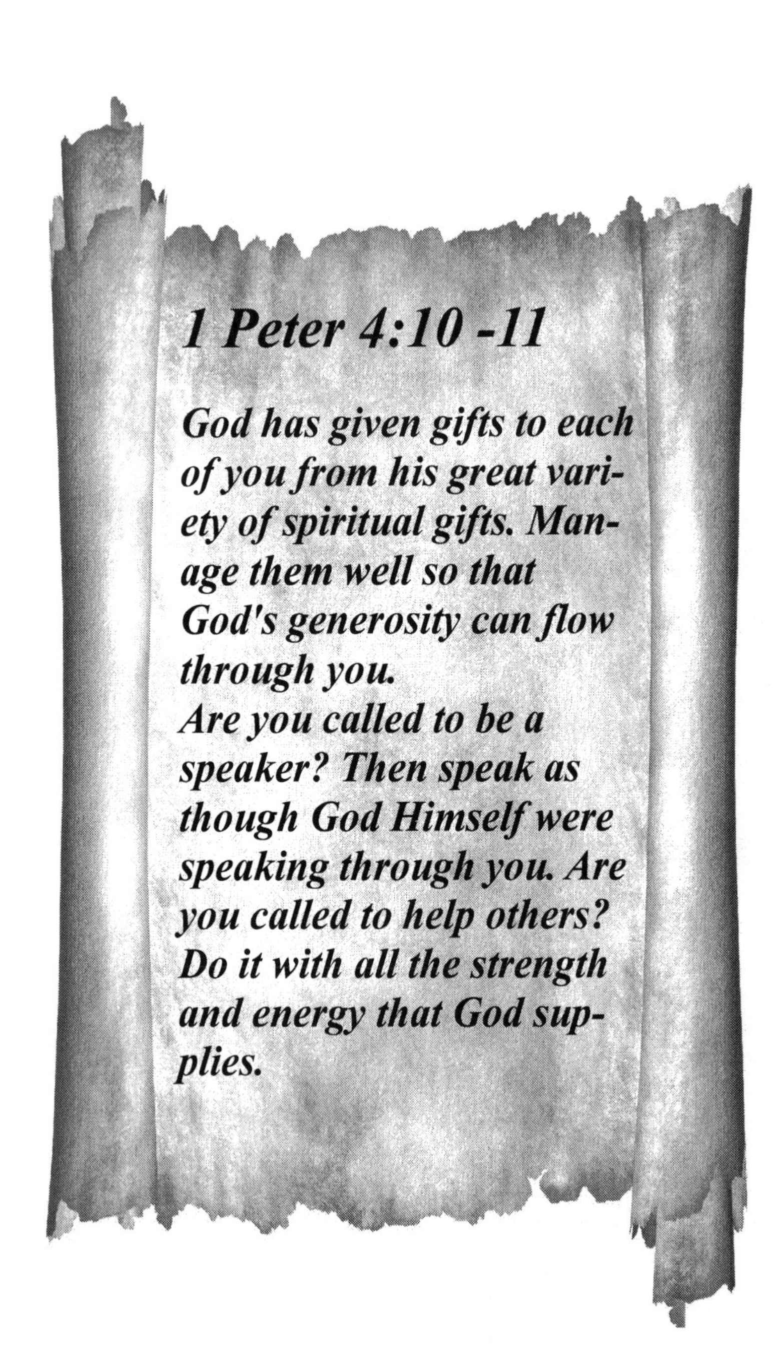
1 Peter 4:10 -11
God has given gifts to each of you from his great variety of spiritual gifts. Manage them well so that God's generosity can flow through you.
Are you called to be a speaker? Then speak as though God Himself were speaking through you. Are you called to help others? Do it with all the strength and energy that God supplies.

TOPIC: Work

*“**God** has **given gifts** to **each of you**”*

Picture God giving beautiful gifts to each of you

The most important point here is that you visualize being given a gift that you will never forget. For example your first bike, first car, engagement ring, or the birth of your first child. Linking this to a special gift you have already received will work even better.

*“from his great variety of **spiritual gifts**”*

while you are driving in a fork lift in His spiritual gifts warehouse

I heard a story once about a man who died and went to Heaven. Jesus was walking around with Him. They came upon a door with the man’s name on it. The man said, “What is in there?” Jesus opened the door. It was full of treasures and wrapped gifts. The man said, “Wow, what is all this?” Jesus replied, “These are all the gifts God had in store for you on Earth that you never opened or used.” This is the association I made when I read this verse. In my mind I actually changed the original story and added me and God getting and using those gifts. This may seem like a large amount of information or details in the link I created. Actually, this whole picture and the changes came to me in literally less than a second. Our brains are amazing at how they know where they want to store information and why.

"Manage them well so that "

and he looks over at you and says, "Manage them well so that..."

Does Management 101 pop into anyone's mind? Perhaps, you see yourself reading a book on "How to Manage God Gifts", or see yourself in a classroom being taught how to manage well.

*"God's **generosity can flow through you"***

While God is still talking, he puts his hand on top of your head and you see the word "generosity" flow through you.

Taking the individual letters or the word and adding action to them is a common way to make links. Links that are out of the ordinary, shocking, humorous, or scary are what make us remember the link better.

*"Are you called to be a **speaker**? "*

And the word turns into a great big speaker over your mouth

Instead of seeing a speaker here, an auditory learner may hear someone asking this question over a loud speaker or megaphone. A kinesthetic learner could be holding the speaker or standing so close they can feel the vibrations.

*"Then **speak** as though **God** himself were **speaking through you**."*

and when you open your mouth God speaks through you

My picture here is God standing next to my ear and speaking directly into it and I am just repeating what He is saying. An alternative image could be your body being a big speaker that is attached to a microphone.

*"Are you called to **help others**?"*

and says, "help others, help others".

This is an auditory learner picture. Visual and kinesthetic learners might visualize helping the people standing around or handing out fliers that read "help others".

*"Do it with all the **strength and energy** that God **supplies**"*

each time he repeats "help others", you get superhero strength and energy supplies building up around you or inside of you

I can see myself growing in superhero strength, my muscles getting huge and my legs running faster. I see a massive amount of boxes labeled energy supplies, similar to energy drinks, being put all around me. Another idea could be to use different keywords and creating different links.

Jabez cried out to the God of Israel, "Oh, that you would bless me and enlarge my territory!" Let your hand be with me, and keep me from harm so that I will be free from pain!" And God granted his request.

TOPIC: Work

“Jabez cried out”

Jabez standing on top of a mountain crying “out”

I see a man dressed in ancient clothes similar to people in the movies with robes on. His hands are in the air and he is calling out in a loud and distressed voiced. Maybe you see Him actually crying with tears on his face.

*“to the **God of Israel**”*

while crying out, he looks up, the clouds start moving, and spell out the words “God of Israel”.

I enjoy the thought of seeing the clouds moving and sending us messages. This is what Dave is referring to when he talks about our brains finding patterns. I exaggerated those patterns and turned the clouds into words.

"Oh, that you would bless me and enlarge my territory!”

Jabez looks down in the valley and sees his livestock is running out of grazing areas and he prays with great fervor, “Oh,

that you would bless me and enlarge my territory!"

I envision Jabez standing on this mountain in great distress, his face red with emotion because he is running out of grazing area, knowing that if he does not expand his territory his animals will become sick and die for lack of good food. I went with an auditory learner style here because it is actually a prayer.

"Let your ***hand*** *be with me,"*

All of a sudden his territory boundaries start to be moved by a huge hand that reaches down from heaven.

I used the keyword hand. Other options might be using hand together with "with me"

"and keep me from ***harm*** *so that I will be* ***free from pain****!"*

On the hand is a large yellow flashing caution sign which flashes "NO Harm, freedom from pain, NO Harm, freedom from pain!"

Once again I stayed with the familiar yellow flashing caution sign meaning no harm. Free from pain was difficult to link. I kept seeing freedom and picturing an American flag. I struggled to get a link that would go to the next keyword with ease. Therefore, I kept the American flag in my mind by putting it as an image over the ground but still being able to see the ground. Next I saw the word Freedom stretched across the flag. Then I applied all of this to the yellow caution sign reading "No harm, free-dom from pain". This may seem complicated but our minds can do this with ease.

"And God ***granted*** *his request."*

Then the sign becomes a huge rubber stamp that stamps the ground "Granted".

Try using different keywords just to practice having different links. There are times when I change the original keyword because the links are not strong enough later for easy recall.

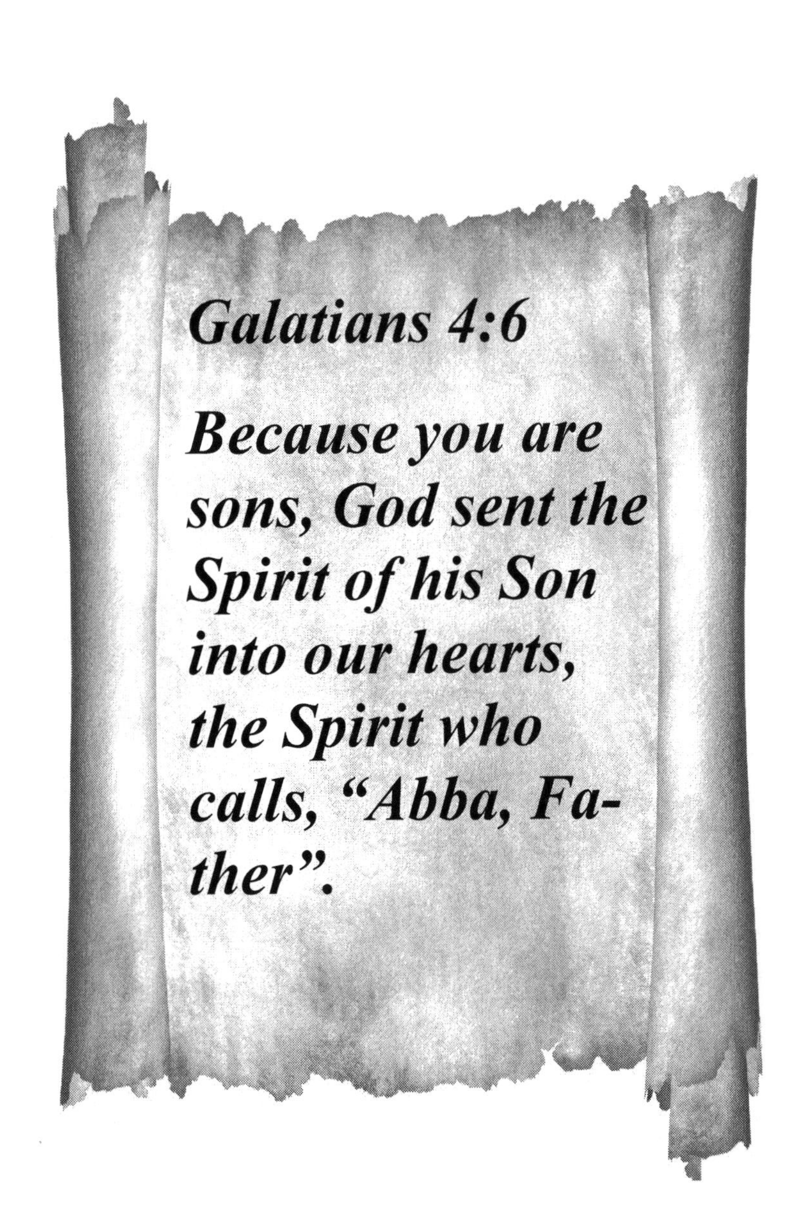
Galatians 4:6
Because you are sons, God sent the Spirit of his Son into our hearts, the Spirit who calls, "Abba, Father".

TOPIC: Family

*"Because you **are sons**"*

Picture the whole earth covered with people all wearing hats that say "U R Sons."

I used an image from texting on my cell phone, UR. Maybe you hear some one saying, "You are sons". Perhaps you see a father and a son or a father and children.

*"God sent the **Spirit** of **his Son** into our **hearts**"*

A huge dove-shaped hat (i.e. the Holy Spirit) descends from the sky and on the front in huge gold letters it reads, "His Son," inside a huge red heart

I used replacing one item for another. The dove symbol of the spirit was replaced by a hat and exaggerated to a hat with wings. Using more than on memory linking step can enhance the strength of the link.

“the ***Spirit*** *who* ***calls****, “****Abba, Father****.”*

And “from the heart, the Holy Spirit calls out, “Abba, Father””

Purposely putting the word “calls” into the link will help you remember call instead of thinking it reads “cried out”, which we also often see in scripture. Maybe this picture is more like someone getting a phone call from Abba Father? Or possibly you feel a strong emotion because God is your Father.

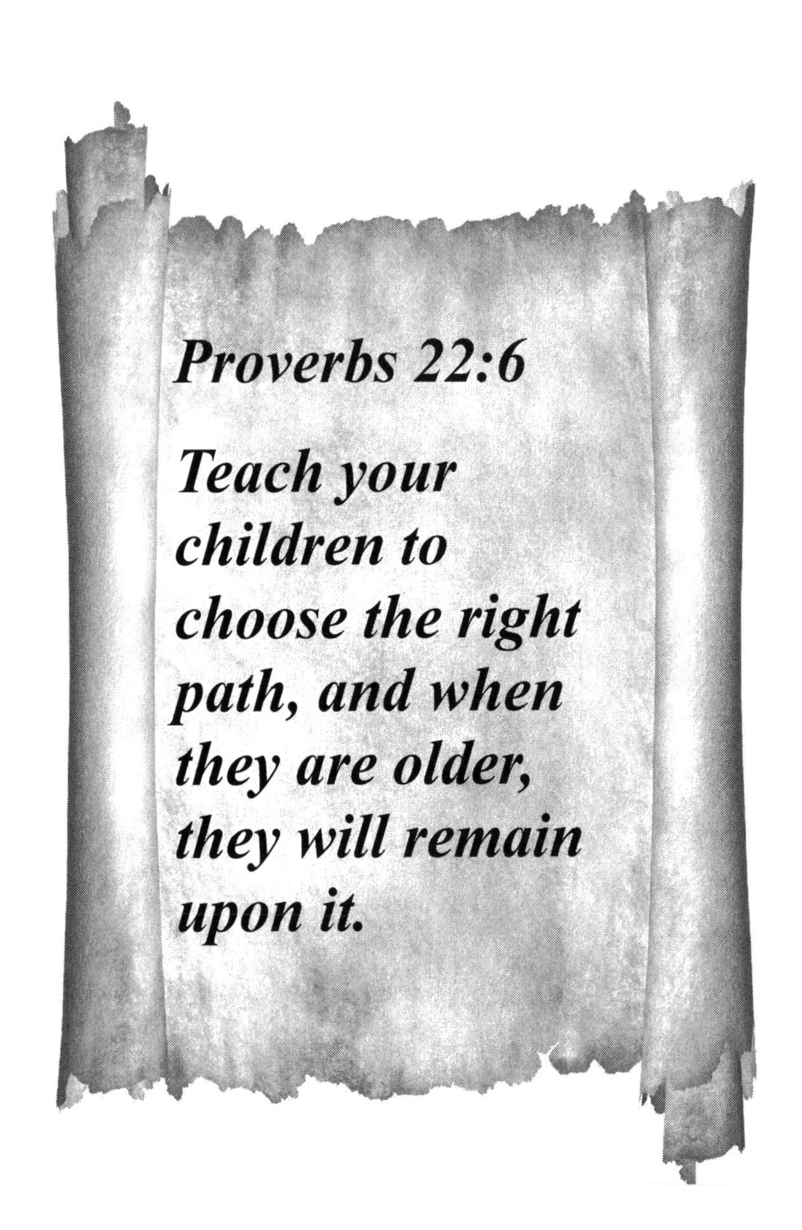
Proverbs 22:6
Teach your
children to
choose the right
path, and when
they are older,
they will remain
upon it.

TOPIC: Family

*"**Teach** your **children** to"*

Picture a group of parents wearing t-shirts that say "Teacher" at a game show yelling behind their children

An alternate story could be seeing yourself or someone else teaching your children.

"choose the right path,"

"choose the right path, choose the right path," (similar to people yelling in the audience at a game show like The Price is Right or Deal or No Deal, etc.)

Continuing the alternate story, before you is a fork in the road, one direction is a golden path and the other direction is a dirt path all full of ruts, holes and weeds.

*"and when they are **older**"*

As the children run towards the right path they become progressively older, (i.e., aging from 5 to 10 to 15 to 20)

Alternate story ideas, seeing a grey haired person as your picture for older, maybe you see your child with children of their own, or heading off to college.

“they will ***remain upon it.****”*

the children are skipping and singing, “I love the golden path its so easy I am going to remain on it”

Alternate story ideas, maybe your path has bumper pads that when you try to leave the path you bounce right back on to it.

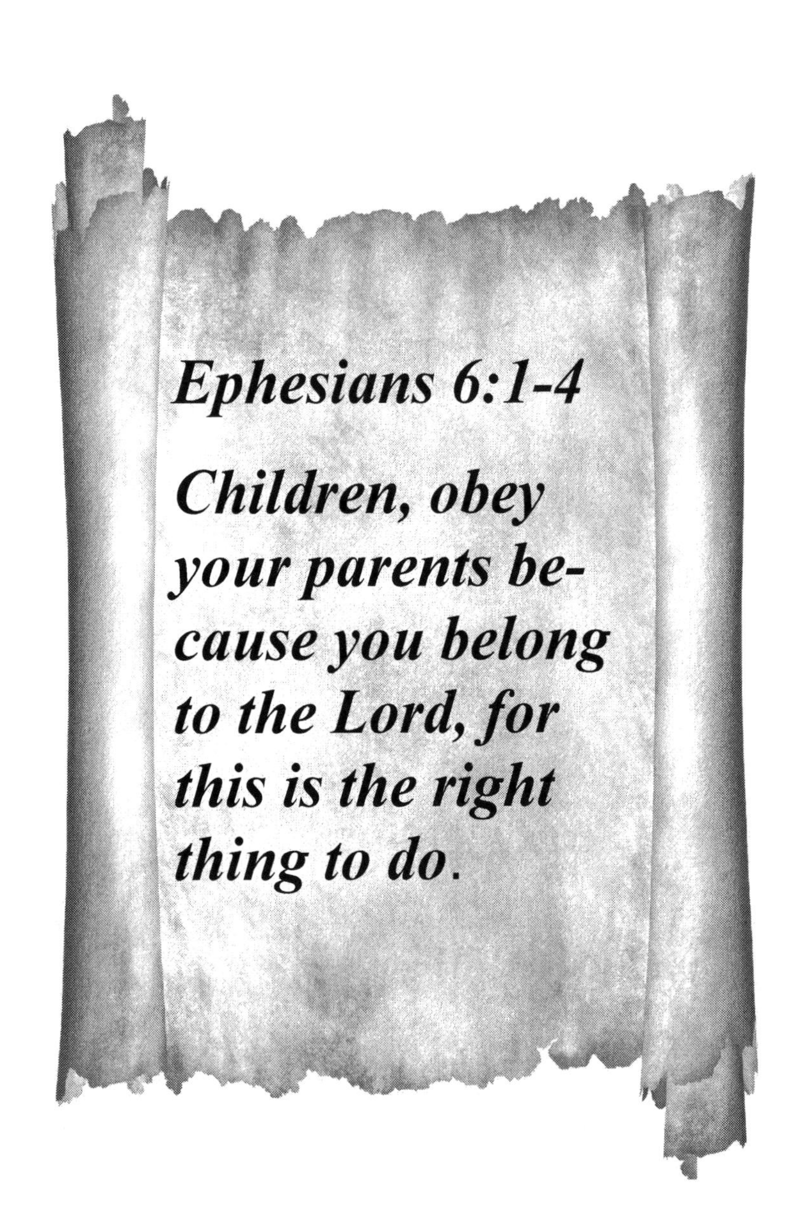
Ephesians 6:1-4
Children, obey your parents because you belong to the Lord, for this is the right thing to do.

TOPIC: Family

"Honor your father and mother." This is the first of the Ten Commandments that ends with a promise.
And this is the promise: If you honor your father and mother, "you will live a long life, full of blessing."
And now a word to you fathers. Don't make your children angry by the way you treat them. Rather, bring them up with the discipline and instruction approved by the Lord.

"Children, obey *your parents"*

As children are getting ready to cross the street a crossing guard is holding a handheld sign which reads, "Obey" instead of "Stop."

An auditory learner may hear someone saying, "Obey your parents". A kinesthetic learner told me when he heard this phrase he thought of getting his knuckles whacked.

"because you ***belong to the Lord"***

as the children are crossing the street the cross guard is saying to them, get-a-

long to the Lord, similar to the tune "get-a-long little doggie, get-a-long"

I changed the word belong to get-a-long, a substitute word, knowing our minds will recall the picture with the tune in it but also remember the verse reads belong to the Lord. Maybe you envision people being stamped "belongs to the Lord" or being hugged and feeling a sense of pride and belonging.

*"for this is the **right** thing to do."*

and pointing to the right.

I actually see a huge flashing arrow pointing to the right. Perchance you are familiar with marching terms and you hear the order "right face!"

"Honor** your **father and mother."

The children turn right and walk into a courtroom and the bailiff says, "All rise for the Honorable Father and Mother,"

This image came to me with great humor. I used to work with kids in the Juvenile Justice System. I can imagine what their faces would look like if their parents were the judge. If you watch court room TV shows, you may have those images coming to your mind. Perhaps you have been before a judge yourself and those images come to mind. Remember that this verse is about God's rules concerning life, not harsh and unjust judgments.

"*This is the first of the* ***Ten Commandments*** *that ends with a* ***promise."***

The bailiff says, "Raise your right hand and put your left hand on the Ten Commandments and promise".

I see this straight out of a court room TV show with the exception that they are holding the Ten Commandments instead of a Bible.

"And this is the ***promise:*** *If you* ***honor*** *your* ***father and mother"***

"Do you promise to tell the truth to the honorable father and mother?"

Can you imagine your children having to go through this the next time they tell differing stories or want to tattle on their sibling? Be careful as you put your links together to remember the word "promise" is used twice.

"you will ***live*** *a* ***long life****,* ***full of blessing****."*

"Our first witness is a lively man with long legs called Life, and our second witness is full of blessing"

Maybe you picture an elderly person for the image long life. People who sign American Sign Language will often exaggerate the signs to get their point across. Exaggerating long life or full of blessing is a great option.

"And now a word to you fathers."

And the Judge says, "and now a word to you Fathers" (this is similar an announcer saying "and now a word from our sponsors")

Maybe you see the mother sitting in the judge's seat now. I changed my image to more of the TV court room type judge. Perhaps you prefer using the image of God being the just judge as He is frequently referred to in the Bible.

*"Don't make your **children angry** by the way you **treat** them"*

The bailiff shows the Fathers exhibit A: In this picture are the children who were angry after bad treatment.

I envisioned a video of children behaving badly as a reaction to their parent frustrating them being played for the Judge. The children reacted by lashing out in anger. Having worked with families for over twenty years, this picture causes a strong negative effect for me. However unpleasant it does make a strong memory link.

“Rather, bring them up”

The honorable Judge says in a deep southern drawl, “Raaaaatherrrrr interesting, bring them up here.”

Once again humor and exaggeration is used to enhance the memory link

*“with the **discipline and instruction approved by the Lord.**”*

After they are brought up, the Judge reads his verdict, “I created a new discipline and instruction approved by the Lord.”

I see the Judge handing the parents a how-to book for their children. The parents are elated at getting such a judgment! I used a lot of keywords for this phrase. It could be just as memorable if only one of two keywords were used.

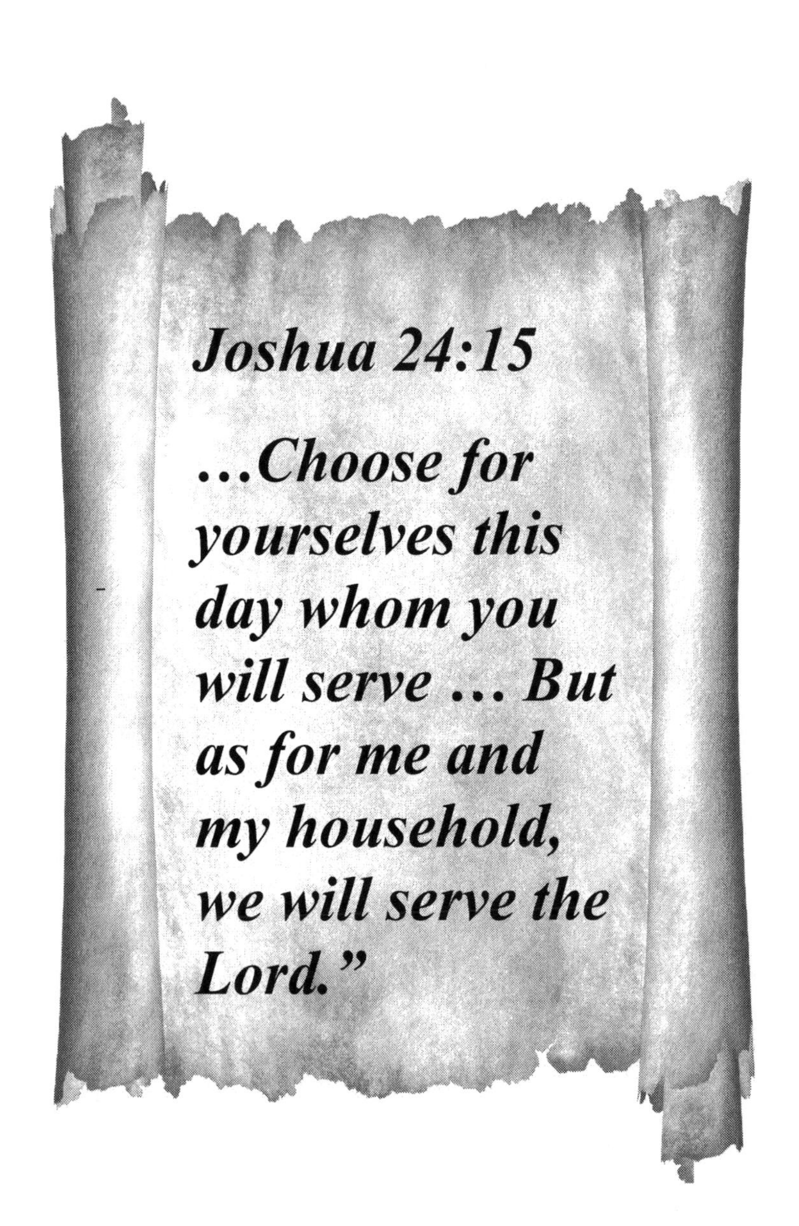
Joshua 24:15
…Choose for yourselves this day whom you will serve … But as for me and my household, we will serve the Lord."

TOPIC: Family

*“**Choose** for yourselves this day whom you will **serve**”*

Flying in the sky is an airplane pulling a banner that reads, “Choose” and the bewildered butler is standing there with his silver serving tray

Sometimes reading the passage that the verse comes from can be helpful in getting the memory links you need to make it rememberable.

*“But as for me and **my household**, we **will serve the Lord**.”*

All of a sudden, a man comes running out of the crowd knocking the serving tray out of the butler’s hands, proclaiming my household will serve the Lord!

This is an auditory learner type memory link. A visual learner may imagine a huge house holding a tray full of food serving the Lord. Maybe you want to personalize it by having you and your family doing something to serve the Lord like worshiping or serving others.

Psalms 139:1-10

TOPIC: Life

Our life with the Lord

Psalms 139:1-10

1. O Lord, you have searched me and you know me.
2. You know when I sit and when I rise; you perceive my thoughts from afar.
3. You discern my going out and my lying down; you are familiar with all my ways.
4. Before a word is on my tongue you know it completely, O Lord.
5. You hem me in—behind and before; you have laid your hand upon me.
6. Such knowledge is too wonderful for me, too lofty for me to attain.
7. Where can I go from your Spirit? Where can I flee from your presence?
8. If I go up to the heavens, you are there; if I make my bed in the depths, you are there.
9. If I rise on the wings of the dawn, if I settle on the far side of the sea,
10. Even there your hand will guide me, your right hand will hold me fast.

“Oh, ***Lord*** *You have* ***searched me”***

The Lord is holding a huge flashlight and searching for me

I see this picture more like flashlight tag. When the light hits you, you have to freeze.
Personal note for grandparents, this works a lot easier because you do not have to run.

“and You ***know*** *me”*

The Lord says, "Oh, I know you"

“You know me” is very abstract, try using a substitute word to help you come up with a picture. Maybe breaking up the words to “no, me?”, “now me?” thinking you are next, or the warm feeling of knowing someone knows you well and loves you just the way you are.

“You know when ***I sit*** *and* ***when I rise”***

I am sitting in a recliner chair then I push the button to rise back up (like a chair that raises up until you are standing on your feet)

I encourage you to go with the first thing that pops into your head.

"*You **perceive** my **thoughts** from **afar**"*

*"You discern my going out and my **lying down**"*

While I am rising up out of the chair little perceptive thought bubbles travel afar, to the Lord. They have all my thoughts in them. Then I walked outside onto my sunny patio to begin lying down on a lounge chair

I went with cartoon images, which is a substitute image, for "perceive my thoughts from afar". It could be just as easy to use only one or two keywords and create different links. Creating images for abstract concepts can take some time. Relaxing and focusing on the phrase works better than getting frustrated or stressed trying to think up a link that works.

*"you are **familiar with all my ways**"*

The Lord comes onto the patio because we're bff's (best friends forever) He is familiar with all my ways.

I put this link in the book because a lady I was working with created it. It worked very well for her because she attached it to deep emotional feelings and exaggeration. The thought of having God be her bff was amazing to her and out of the ordinary.

*“**Before** a **word** is on **my tongue**, you **know it completely**, Oh Lord”*

The Lord looks at me intently and sees cartoon-animated words dancing in my head before they reach my tongue and He knows it completely

Perhaps you see a computer type image going on in your head. A mistake I have often seen with this phrase is the person making the link misses the word before and has the word on their tongue instead.

*“You **hem me in**, **behind and before**”*

He leans over and says, "You look cold, let me put these beach towels around you" and He hems me in with a big beach towel behind me and before me and sews up the sides so I'm warm

This memory link is from a visual learner. I remember her link and mine at the same time. My link is based on a sermon I preached years ago. The phrase “you hem me in” is a common phrase referring to war. The image refers to a king in the middle of his army protected on all sides. Creating memory links with other learning styles is not only fun but can be strengthening for your links.

*"You have **laid** Your **hand upon me**"*

He lays His hand upon me and asks, "Is that ok?"

Imagine the incredible feeling of love and acceptance you would feel if Our Sovereign Lord put his hand on you. It would probably be better than the President or a famous person shaking your hand. Simply picturing a hand being put on you or someone may not be strong enough for a memory link. Adding a picture that generates strong emotion can strengthen the link.

*"Such **knowledge** is too **wonderful** for me"*

His hand turns into a floating Book of Knowledge, flashing the word "wonderful" on the cover.

Using the image of a Bible, encyclopedia or something that represents knowledge and can easily be linked to wonderful is the key here.

*"too **lofty** for me to attain"*

The lofty floating Book of Knowledge goes higher and higher into the sky, I try to grab it, but I can't reach it (similar to trying to catch a wind blown feather)

If you can not come up with a picture for this phrase remember that not all of the phrases have to have links. Some phrases are better to just remember.

*"Where can I go from your **Spirit**? Where can I flee from your **presence**?"*

The Book of Knowledge changes into a hot air balloon with a huge name Spiritual Presence printed on it.

Because I have ridden in a hot air balloon this connection was easy for me. Using personal experiences and connecting them to your memory link is a great and fun way to put memory links together. Another possible alternate story here could be the parallel story of Jonah fleeing from God.

*"If I **go up to the heavens**, you are **there**"*

I jump up and grab the hot air balloon named Spiritual Presence and we begin to go up to the heavens and I look out and see a cloud formation that reads UR There

There are times when I change the proper verbiage or grammar for the sake of knowing the right key-words in the phrase. As in this example instead of going up into the sky I am going up into the heav-ens. Our brain will do the rest to make it clear when necessary.

*"If **I make my bed** in the **depths**, you are **there**."*

As the balloon begins to descend I make my bed and in the depths of a voice I hear "UR There"

In the depths was a hard link for me. I did not come up with any thing. I decide to look the word up in the dictionary. One of the definitions refers to being tonal; "in the depth of his voice" Using extra helps like the dictionary or a thesaurus are great tools for getting memory links.

*“If **I rise** on the **wings of the dawn**”*

I rise up to see where the voice comes from and I see the wings of the dawn which look like a humongous eagle, I jump onto the wings

Some other ideas here could be something similar to hang gliding or maybe you only have “dawn” as a keyword and make a link related to the dawn.

*“if I **settle** on the **far side of the sea**,”*

as I fly on the wings of the dawn, I settle in for the ride to the far side of the sea

Once again you might go back to story of Jonah who thought he could ride this boat far away on the sea. Maybe you think of the world’s first settlers far across the sea.

*“Even there your **hand** will **guide me** your right hand will hold me fast.”*

I land on the far side of the sea. A huge wave in the shape of God’s Hand guides

me, and holds me fast.

I used exaggeration- the huge wave, action- the fast moving wave, personification- having the wave be God's hand and personalization- by having God's hand hold me. By using so many memory link options I created a strong and unforgettable image and memory link.

1 Peter 5:7
Cast all your anxiety on him because he cares for you.

TOPIC: Anxiety

*“**Cast** all your **anxiety** on him”*

Jesus, the Fisher of Men, has a huge fishing pole and is casting his line to catch your anxiety,

I considered many different ideas here and finally settled on this one. My first impression was fishing, how to link fishing to anxiety took a little more work. Be encouraged to keep looking for the best and strongest link.

*“because he **cares for you**”*

like fish on a stringer line, he carries anxiety for you.

Maybe you see Him caring for you because you are hurt. I have heard others say they pictured Him acting like a nurse caring for people.

Philippians 4:6-7

Do not be anxious about anything, but in everything, by prayer and petition, with thanksgiving, present your requests to God. And the peace of God, which transcends all understanding, will guard your hearts and your minds in Christ Jesus.

TOPIC: Anxiety

*"Do **not** be **anxious** about any- thing, but in everything,"*

Entering a church there is a big sign on the door with the universal "No" symbol, Ø, over the word anxiety,

Once you have an image or picture for a certain word like this verse has the word, "no" try to stay with it as often as you can. As time goes by you will be able to make memory links faster by having a large repertoire of images already linked.

*"by **prayer** and **petition**, with thanksgiving, **present** your re- quests **to God**."*

under the word anxiety the sign reads "Sign here: Prayer Petition to Present to God".

There are four keywords in this link. Some times less is better. Try it first with only one or two. When you go back over the verse if you forget a phrase then add and link more keywords.

*"And the **peace** of **God**,"*

Then God sends his peace, i.e. the Holy Spirit dove, and it lands on your head...

The peace of God is completely subject to each person's opinion. I went with the Biblical reference, "and the Holy Spirit descended on him in bodily form like a dove."

*"which **transcends** all under-standing, will **guard your hearts and** your **minds** in Christ **Jesus**."*

it transcends into a suit of armor to guard your heart and mind, and the ar-mor is stamped "belongs to Jesus".

The word "transcends" is very abstract, using a sub-stitute word or image will work best. Another idea for "guard your hearts and minds" is possibly having an actual guard stand over you.

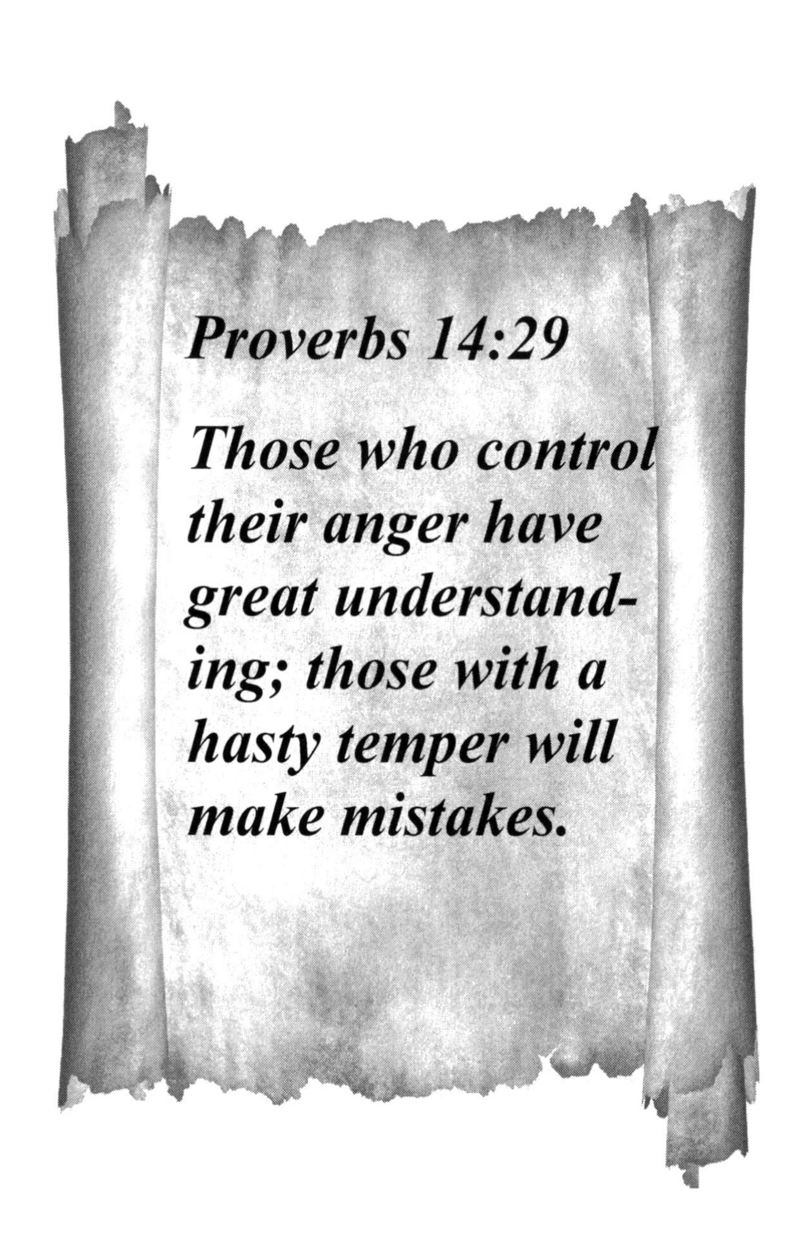
Proverbs 14:29
Those who control their anger have great understanding; those with a hasty temper will make mistakes.

TOPIC: Anger

"Those who ***control*** *their* ***anger*** *have* ***great understanding****;"*

Swooping in, like Superman or Mighty Mouse, to control the angry crowd is my superhero GREAT UNDERSTANDING!

Alternate story could be having the letters a-n-g-e-r running around and the words control and understanding trying to lasso them like animals at a rodeo.

"those with a ***hasty temper*** *will make* ***mistakes"***

and He hastily knocks over the temperature gauge, as it falls just missing the fresh cooked steaks

Okay I admit it I was starting to get hungry when I came up with this one! Another idea is having the words interacting with each other. Or possibly personalizing the phrase to a time when you had a hasty temper and made mistakes.

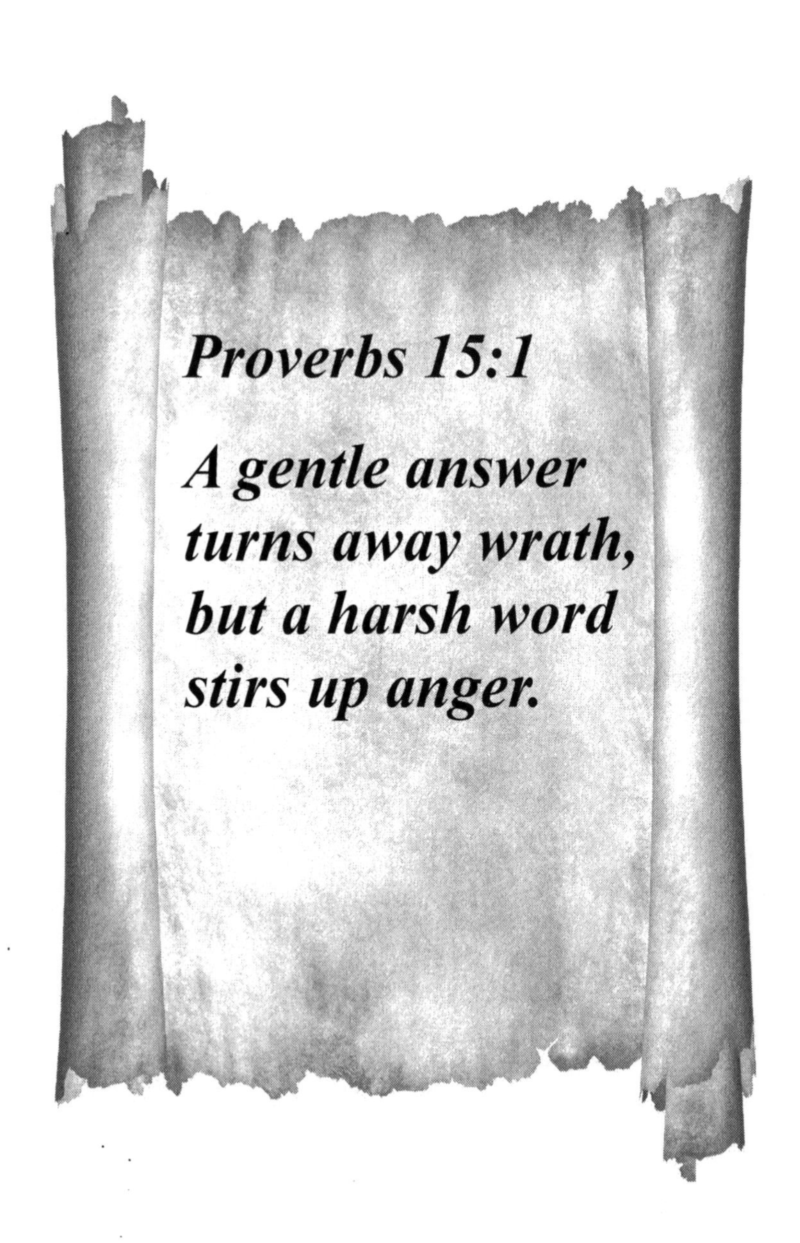
Proverbs 15:1
A gentle answer
turns away wrath,
but a harsh word
stirs up anger.

TOPIC: Anger

*"A **gentle answer turns away wrath**,"*

Gentle answers the door and says "Yo! turn away, Wrath dude!"

Being an auditory learner I had a lot of fun with these words. Some possible visuals could be see-ing a gentle lamb, or a gentle wind some how inter-acting with wrath. A suggestion I was told was hav-ing a gentle wind blowing the leaves on the tree of wrath as opposed to the tree of life.

*"but a **harsh** word **stirs** up **anger**"*

Harsh comes in and yells, "Let's stir some anger up!!!"

Another idea here is, while stirring your alphabet soup you see a harsh word...Anger! Using exag-geration or replacing one item for another may be helpful with this verse.

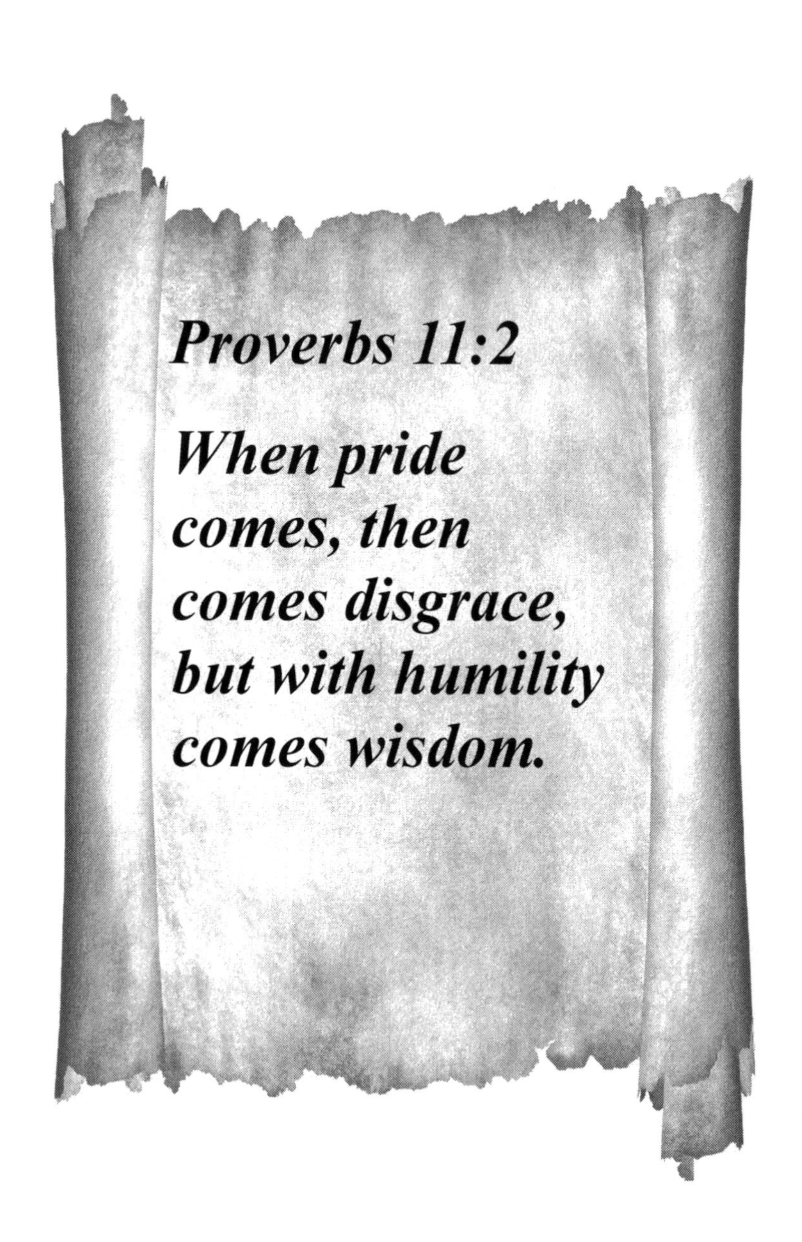
Proverbs 11:2
When pride
comes, then
comes disgrace,
but with humility
comes wisdom.

TOPIC: Pride

"When pride comes"

You are entering a Masquerade ball when Pride comes dressed as Marie Antoinette or maybe a Kanye West

Because all of the keywords are abstract in this verse focus on each keyword and go with your first impression. Then add actions, personalizations, and etc. I used costumes over my abstract word which reminded me of certain historical figures. The weakness to using historical figures is different people have different opinions about them or may not know who they are.

"then comes disgrace"

and then comes disgrace dressed as Benedict Arnold.

"but with humility"

But with humility dressed as Mother Theresa

"comes wisdom"

comes wisdom dressed as Albert Einstein.

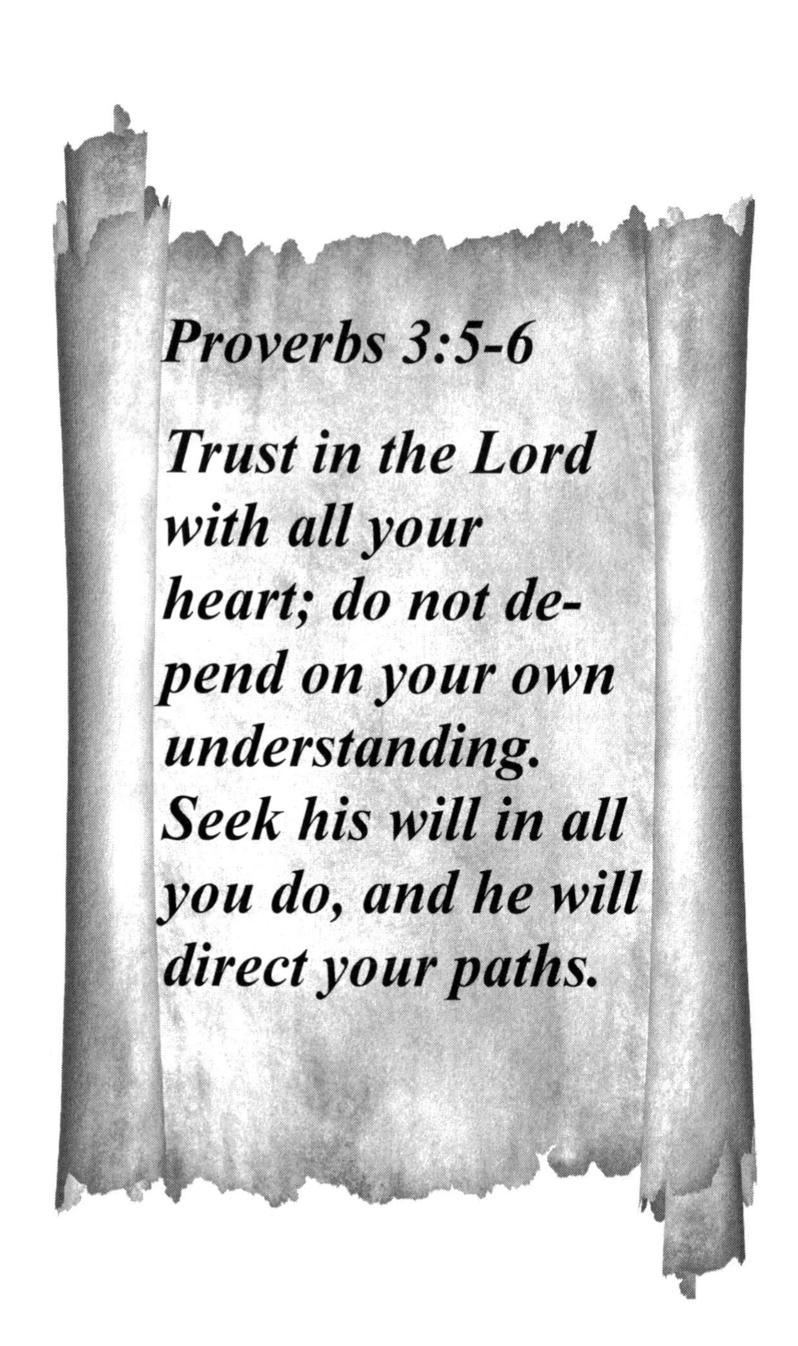
Proverbs 3:5-6
Trust in the Lord with all your heart; do not depend on your own understanding. Seek his will in all you do, and he will direct your paths.

TOPIC: Trust

*“**Trust** in the **Lord** with **all your heart**;”*

In the bank vault, there is a huge safe made by Trust-Lord Company and you put in the safe all of your heart,

The heart image here can be paper hearts or visualizing a real heart. Try to find a strong image.

*“do **not** depend on **your own understanding**.”*

In order to make enough room in the safe for your heart you must remove your own understanding

I pictured having to take my brain out. Instead you might have to take out all of your books, or degrees.

*“**Seek his will** in all you do”*

Once your own understanding is out of the way you start seeking his will “where is that will anyways?”

I went with the action of seeking for a legal Will document. Exaggeration could be an interesting option for this phrase.

"and he will ***direct your paths"***

and you find the will directly in your path

I saw a room full of papers and have to zig-zag to get around the room and the Will was laying there in my path. Making this personal could be a very powerful memory link too. For example, having God literally directing you as you travel the path of life.

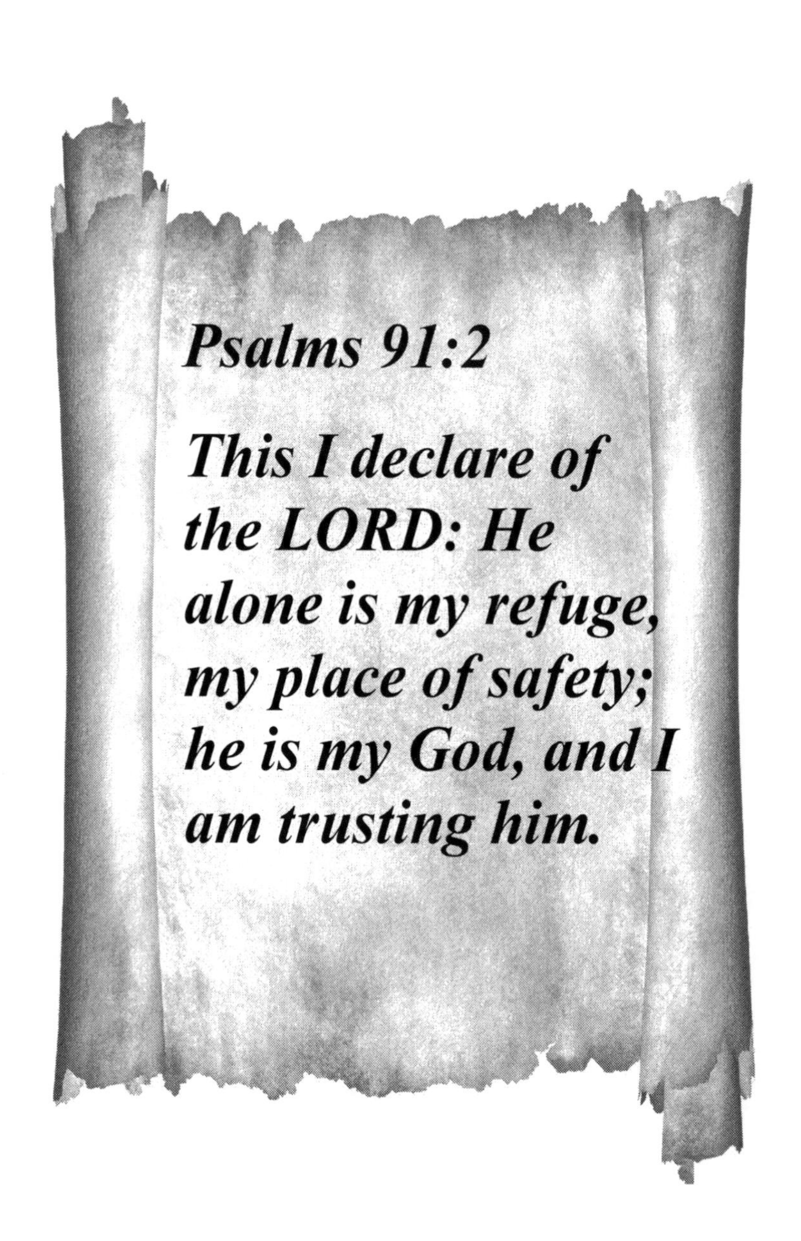
Psalms 91:2
This I declare of the LORD: He alone is my refuge, my place of safety; he is my God, and I am trusting him.

TOPIC: Trust

*"This **I declare** of the **LORD**"*

I do deeclaare!, Said in a southern drawl, The word "Lord" is stretched across the sky

As an auditory learner I love hearing different accents. If you are an auditory person, have fun putting different accents and songs into your memory links. A visual person may read a declaration written about the Lord. The kinesthetic person may be making the declaration.

*"He alone is **my refuge**, my place of safety;"*

The letter R in the word Lord has a door in it; there is a sign on the door which reads "my refuge"

I used a picture which you have seen before of having a door in a word that links one keyword to the next.

*"he is **my God**"*

I open the door and much to my surprise, there is my God!

Just think of how awesome it would be to be able to see God in all his radiant glory standing right in front of you. Moses was not allowed to see God's face because he would die. This is the picture I see with this phrase.

*"and **I am trusting him**"*

I start dancing around with my God singing, "I am trusting Him!"

Find an image that clearly portrays trust. For me it is more of a feeling than a picture. Maybe you see a loving parent or person that you trust. Possibly you see the word trust and that works well enough.

About the Authors

Dave Farrow:

is the current Guinness World Record holder for GREATEST MEMORY! He memorized and recalled the order of 59 decks of cards randomly shuffled together. That's 3,068 cards! He's been featured in over 1000 interviews, including The 700 Club, CNN, Fox News, The Discovery Channel, and Live With Regis and Kelly, to name a few. Dave is a popular speaker for business professionals, students and corporations across North America. Dave has also used his own techniques to become a self-taught expert in nanotechnology, speaking to experts in the field and is currently involved in a US patent filing for a medical testing device that will change the way HIV is tested in developing countries.

Kellie Ann Peterson BS, MFT:

has over 20 years experience working with families: as a pre-school teacher, home-schooling parent, professional nanny, pastoral counseling minister, short-term missionary, and family intervention specialist. She has worked with at-risk youths, families in crisis, reunification of incarcerated parents and their children, and taught parenting classes in correctional facilities. She is a parenting instructor and wrote the current parenting curriculum for the NM Works Program, Welfare to Work, at Central New Mexico's Community College. In addition she is a Parent Coach and Farrow Memory Speaker and Trainer. She speaks regularly at churches teaching memory techniques. She and her husband live in New Mexico, have four grown children and six grandchildren.

Made in the USA
Charleston, SC
22 April 2010